COWARDLY
CLYDE

HOUGHTON MIFFLIN COMPANY   BOSTON

BILL PEET

To Dr. Royce Simpson
with appreciation for
his years of patience
and kindness in caring
for our beloved pets

Copyright © 1979 by William B. Peet

Library of Congress Cataloging in Publication Data

Peet, Bill.
    Cowardly Clyde.

    SUMMARY: For a war horse, Clyde is an abysmal coward,
but he finally decides that even if he isn't brave he can
at least act brave.
    [1. Courage—Fiction. 2. Horses—Fiction]
I. Title.
PZ7.P353Co   [E]   78-24343

ISBN: 0-395-27802-3
ISBN: 0-395-36171-0 (pbk.)

Printed in the United States of America
WOZ   20   19   18   17   16   15   14   13   12

Once there was a brave young knight known as Sir Galavant who rode around on a great war-horse shouting, "Bring on the fire-breathing dragons! Bring on the man-eating giants! Bring on the ogres and trolls! I'll clobber the brutes, I will!"

All the shouting was upsetting to Clyde, the great war-horse. He wasn't the least bit brave, and he worried about what he would do if Sir Galavant ever got his wish and met some horrible monster in a fight to the finish.

Clyde didn't want anyone to know he was a coward, so he pretended to be brave by prancing around with his chest out and his nose in the air. But his uppity act didn't fool the farm dogs. They could spot a coward a mile away and always had great fun barking at the jittery horse just to watch his eyes roll and his ears twitch.

Clyde was so skittish that even a cross-eyed silly old scarecrow gave him the creeps. And when he heard the news that a gigantic ogre was on the rampage far out in the countryside, the faint-hearted horse was horrified.

The monster always attacked in the middle of the night, kicking in barn doors and ripping off rooftops to get at the livestock. It was a time of terror for the farmers and their families, and since they had no way to fight the huge beast, they decided to abandon their farms and flee to some faraway place.

They scurried down the roads by the hundreds, taking their animals and all the things they could possibly cart or carry along with them.

"Here! Here! No need to panic!" shouted the brave Sir Galavant. "Don't lose your heads! I'll throttle the monster in a trice! I'll finish him off before tea time!"

"No! No! Not that easy!" warned an old farmer. "I got a peek at the monster last night. He's a whopper of a thing. A giant owl-eyed ox-footed ogre, nearly as big as a barn. A night-prowlin' beast who never shows himself in broad daylight. *Never!* They say he hides out by day far back in the woods to the north of here. But anyone who dared go in after him would be a dim-witted noodlehead!"

"Then I'm a dim-witted noodlehead," laughed Sir Galavant, "and I'm off to meet the owl-eyed ogre. Gee! Hup! Clyde, boy! Let's go!"

As Clyde galloped on north across the fields and cow pastures he was hoping they would never find the ogre, or even a sign of him. But pretty soon, to the horse's dismay, they came upon a barn with half the roof ripped off, and all around the barn were the huge two-toed tracks of the monster.

"He must be a whopper!" exclaimed Sir Galavant. "With tracks like these we'll catch up to the beast in no time. Clyde, boy! We're in luck!"

They followed the ogre's tracks on across a grassy meadow until they disappeared into the dark gloomy woods. They were about to enter the woods when Clyde thought of the farmer's grim warning, and a cold shiver ran through him that left his knees so weak and wobbly he staggered to a halt.

"Ho! Ho! Come now!" scoffed Sir Galavant. "Don't tell me my noble high-stepping steed has turned into a chicken!"

No horse can stand to be called a chicken, not even such a cowardly one as Clyde. So with an angry snort he headed on into the gloomy woods.

It was ever so quiet in the woods, with no sign of a bird or a squirrel. The only sound was the "clumpity clumping" of Clyde's big feet. And as they went along through the dark, the brush became so dense they lost the monster's tracks, but they could still follow the scattering of bones left from the ogre's feasting.

Then pretty soon a "huffling snuffling" noise echoed through the trees like the breathing of some gigantic thing.

"The time has come," muttered Sir Galavant, clamping his visor shut and getting a good grip on his sword. And, all at once, there in the deep shadows was the terrible ogre!

The great hulking beast was sprawled out on his back in the oak trees, sound asleep and snoring.

"What a cinch," whispered the knight. "The brute is far off in dreamland, out of this world. I could slit his gullet in a twinkling, and

he'd never know it. But that wouldn't be sporting, would it, Clyde,
boy? Not fair at all."

Then, to the horse's horror and amazement, Sir Galavant shouted,
"En garde!"

The startled monster reared up with an angry "Whurf!" his fierce
owl eyes searching everywhere at once. "Wheeeefle!!" he gleefully
squealed when he spied the knight on horseback, right under his
great horned snout. The greedy ogre was always hungry enough to
eat a horse, and also a knight in armor, saddle and all.

And he leaped to the attack just as Sir Galavant lashed out with his sword. But they both missed when Clyde swerved to one side to escape the terrible claws. Then the panicky horse was off and away, running through the woods at a furious gallop.

"Whoa! Whoa! Hold up!" shouted Sir Galavant. "Stop! Stop! You chicken-livered cowardly big lout!"

But the worst of all insults couldn't stop Clyde now.

He was determined to save both of their necks whether his fool-hardy master liked it or not. And he kept going full gallop, dodging past tree limbs, leaping over boulders and logs, out of the spooky old woods.

Clyde was far out in the meadow before he dared slow down to catch his breath. Then, as he took a look back to make sure they weren't being followed, he suddenly discovered his saddle was empty! Sir Galavant was gone! He had taken a tumble, way back in the woods somewhere! Clyde was more frantic than ever! For all he knew the poor fellow had already been devoured by the ogre. Yet the horse would never know unless he went back into the woods to find out, and he wasn't half brave enough to do that.

"If there's even a slim chance," thought Clyde, "that I could do something to save him, then I must take the chance. If I'm not half brave enough, then I must pretend to be brave! I'll put on a big act!"

Then snorting fiercely, just like a high-spirited steed, Clyde went charging headlong back into the gloomy old woods.

When Clyde reached the spot where they had first met the monster
he was stopped short by a great roaring burst of laughter, "Gur-hoof!
Gur-hoof! Gur-hoof!" The giant beast was in a frolicsome mood,
playing the old cat-and-mouse game. And the mouse was Sir Galavant!

Even though he had no chance of winning, the heroic young knight put up a furious fight, swinging away with his sword, while the ogre kept jabbing at him with a claw that sent him sprawling. Clyde knew the game could end in a second with one crunching bite unless a horse got into the game.

25

To get the monster's attention Clyde suddenly sank his teeth into his scaly blue tail. "Garf!" cried the ogre, who was much more surprised than hurt. He had never been bitten before, and he whirled around in a snarling fury.

Then, as Clyde turned to run, the ogre forgot about the knight, and in great leaps and bounds came chasing after Clyde, just as the horse had expected him to.

Once again Clyde was galloping away through the woods, but this time not nearly so fast. He was getting leg-weary after so much running, and the ogre was surprisingly quick for such a big, clumsy, ox-footed thing.

He came whuffling and gruffling on through the trees, gaining with every giant step. Then in one wild grab he caught the horse by the tail.

That would have been the finish for poor Clyde if he hadn't reached the edge of the woods. In one last desperate lunge, one tremendous surge of horsepower, he made it out into the meadow and hauled the huge ogre out after him.

Suddenly it was the ogre's turn to be terrified. He had been caught by surprise, out in broad daylight with the sun glaring down at him.

An owl-eyed monster who thrives on darkness and gloom can't last ten seconds in the bright sunlight, and he knew it. He let go of the horse and burst into horrible howls and screeches that could be heard all the way to Twickenham.

Sir Galavant came dashing out of the woods just in time to see the monster explode in one big KER–PUFFLE! And just like that he was gone!

"C-C-Clyde!" stammered the flabbergasted knight. "Di-did you see that?!!! The big brute's gone! Vanished! Gone in one big KER–PUFFLE! Amazing! Fantastic! I must spread the great news! Tell everyone! Come on, Clyde! GEE! Hup! Let's go!"

As Sir Galavant sent Clyde racing across the countryside to catch up with the frightened farmers, he suddenly realized they would never believe that such a huge beast could vanish in one big KER–PUFFLE! So he quickly made up a better ending for the ogre.

"Hear this! Hear this!" he shouted. "I have clobbered the monster! Slashed him to bits and pieces! Just one big banquet for the buzzards!!! He's gone forever!"

The wonderful news was greeted with resounding cheers and shouts of joy that echoed for miles around, and Sir Galavant became an instant hero.

After that, when Clyde went prancing along with his chest out and his nose in the air, he *really was* feeling brave. The farm dogs could sense it at once, and they gave up barking at him. It was no fun barking at a horse who won't twitch an ear, or even bat an eye. But after all, a horse who bites a giant ogre on the tail and lives to trot another day is just about as brave as anyone can be.